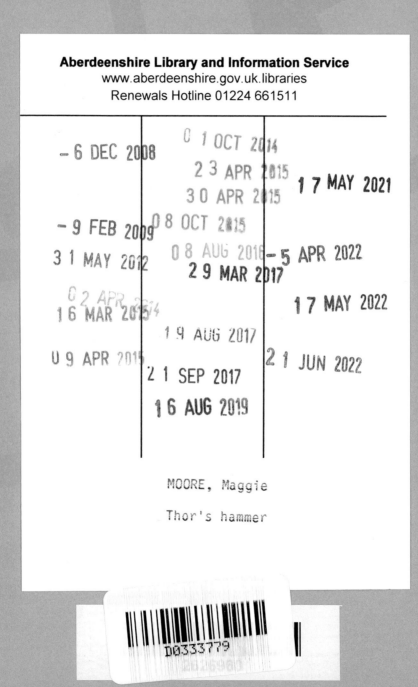

MOORE, Maggie

Thor's hammer

Thor's
Hammer

First published in 2008 by
Franklin Watts
338 Euston Road
London
NW1 3BH

Franklin Watts Australia
Level 17/207 Kent Street
Sydney
NSW 2000

A CIP catalogue record for this book is available
from the British Library.

ISBN 978 0 7496 7997 2 (hbk)
ISBN 978 0 7496 8005 3 (pbk)

Series Editor: Melanie Palmer
Series Advisor: Dr Barrie Wade
Series Designer: Peter Scoulding

Printed in China

Franklin Watts is a division of
Hachette Children's Books,
an Hachette Livre UK company
www.hachettelivre.co.uk

HOPSCOTCH MYTHS

Thor's Hammer

by Maggie Moore and Tim Archbold

FRANKLIN WATTS
LONDON•SYDNEY

Thor woke up with a nasty shock.

"Who's taken my hammer?"

he said, angrily.

5

Everyone was scared. Thor's mighty hammer was magic. It kept them safe from evil giants.

7

"Only a wicked giant could have stolen it," said Loki. "I'll go and find out where it is."

Loki used his magical powers to change into a bird. He flew swiftly to the land of the giants.

Thrym, king of the giants, stood at the entrance to the giants' lair. "What do you want?" he boomed. "Thor's hammer," Loki replied.

"Thor can only have it back if
Freya marries me," said Thrym.

Loki flew back to find Freya.

She was the most beautiful

of all the goddesses.

12

"Thrym will keep Thor's hammer
until you marry him," said Loki.
"I won't marry an ugly, old giant,"
cried Freya.

"I want my hammer and I'll get it back," growled Thor. "Freya, you will not go to Thrym, I will!"

Thor ordered a bridal dress and veil large enough to fit him.

When it was ready, he put on the
dress and covered his face with
the veil. Everyone laughed.

16

"Don't worry," said Thor.
"Giantesses are all ugly,
so I will look beautiful."

Loki and Thor travelled to Thrym's lair. "Welcome, my beautiful bride," said Thrym. "I have prepared a wedding feast for you. But first, let me see your face."

"No," said Loki, "not until the wedding. She is very shy."

They all sat down to eat the feast.
Thor ate an ox, eight salmon
and a goat.

21

He drank two barrels of beer. "She

is hungry and thirsty!" said Thrym.

"Yes," said Loki. "She has been so
nervous about the wedding that she
hasn't eaten or drunk for a week."

Thrym smiled. "Lower your veil, Freya, so that I can see your eyes," he said.

Thor lowered his veil a little.

His red, fiery eyes peered out.

"Her eyes are very red," said Thrym.
"Oh yes," said Loki. "She hasn't
slept for a week either."

"I think it is time to marry
now," said Thrym, smiling.
"We need the hammer first,"
said Loki. "It will bring luck!"

Thrym grumbled, but went to get the hammer. He held it up to celebrate the wedding day.

Thor grabbed the hammer. Then he ripped off his veil and gown. "This is my hammer!" he roared.

There was a great battle. Thor
hurled the hammer at Thrym and
killed him. No giant was left alive!

Thor and Loki returned home as heroes. "No one will ever take my hammer again," Thor promised.

Hopscotch has been specially designed to fit the requirements of the Literacy Framework. It offers real books by top authors and illustrators for children developing their reading skills. There are 63 Hopscotch stories to choose from:

* hardback